No, No, Kitten!

Shelley Moore Thomas

Illustrations by
Lori Nichols

BOYDS MILLS PRESS
AN IMPRINT OF HIGHLIGHTS
Honesdale, Pennsylvania

Boyds Mills Press
An Imprint of Highlights
815 Church Street
Honesdale, Pennsylvania 18431

Printed in Malaysia
ISBN: 978-1-62091-631-5
Library of Congress Control Number: 2014945490

First edition
Designed by Anahid Hamparian
Production by Margaret Mosomillo
The text of this book is set in Courier Prime.
The illustrations are done in dip pen and ink and colorized digitally.
10 9 8 7 6 5 4 3 2 1

For the children of Jefferson Elementary School
—SMT

For Mrs. Eaton, and all the wonderful
teachers at Shades Cahaba Elementary,
who taught my girls to embrace
their imaginations
—LN

Kitten wants a basket.

Kitten wants a pillow.

Kitten wants a blanket.

Kitten wants...

...a puppy.

A puppy?
No, no, no, Kitten.
You cannot have a puppy.
You are a cat!
Cats do not have pets.

Kitten wants some milk.

Kitten wants some catnip.

Kitten wants some fish.

Kitten wants...

A helmet?

No, no, no, Kitten.
You cannot have a helmet.
You are a cat!
Cats do not wear helmets.

Kitten wants a ball.

Kitten wants a string.

Kitten wants a squeaky mouse.

Kitten wants...

...engines, gadgets, and lasers.

Engines, gadgets, and lasers?

No, no, no, Kitten.
You cannot have engines,
gadgets, and lasers.
You are a cat!
Cats play with soft toys,
not engines, gadgets, and lasers.

Kitten wants to creep.

Kitten wants to pounce.

Kitten wants to leap.

Kitten wants...

...to blast off to **Jupiter.**

Jupiter?

No, no, no, Kitten.
You cannot blast
off to Jupiter.
You are a cat!
Cats stay on their
fluffy pillows.
Cats do not go to outer space.

See, Kitten? You can have these:

Not these:

Okay?

Hey, Kitten, what are you doing?

10...9...8...

What's that counting?!

7...6...

Drop that astronaut helmet!

5...4...

Bring that puppy back here!

3...2...

ZIP! ZIP! ZIP!

Zip! Zip! Zip!

Come back by the count of three...

1...

2...

2 ½...

Kitten?

Wow, you did it!

Puppy wants a bowl.

Puppy wants some kibble.

Puppy wants a bone.

Puppy wants...

...a dinosaur.